Picture Purrfect

Kittens

BY MASARU MIZOBUTI and ERIKA TATIHARA

BARRON'S

"I've done a great job drawing this cute little kitten. I'll stop for today and finish the rest of the picture tomorrow," says the artist.

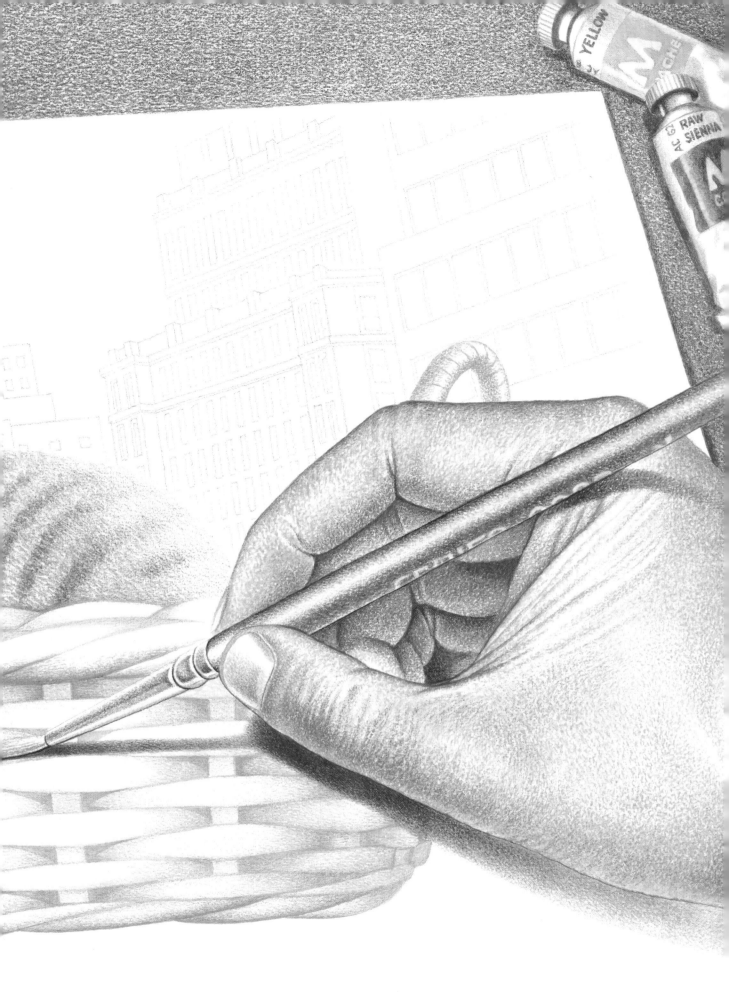

"Sleep well, kitty cat. Oh! I have an idea. I'll give you a name. Hmmm . . . Sam! Yes, your name is going to be Sam. Good night, Sam."

After the artist has gone, Sam opens his eyes wide. "Where am I?"

Sam gets up and looks around. "I have to find out where I am, what kind
of place this is." He starts walking around.

Then Sam climbs onto the windowsill, and sees the big city spread far below. "Wow! I'm almost dizzy. And how noisy it is!" Slowly and carefully, Sam climbs down from the windowsill.

"Honk honk, vroom vroom," the traffic roars. "Shout, shout, yell, yell," the people holler. "Oompah, oompahpah," the music booms. Everything in town seems to be howling at once.

Sam decides to go down to the street. But all he can see are people's feet. Feet everywhere. All the feet are moving very fast and in all directions.

"Isn't there anything better?"
Sam walks along very carefully, so that he won't get stepped on or kicked.

There, on the side of the street, he sees a pile of garbage. "Ugh! How dirty and smelly!" As Sam stares at the mess with disbelief, a stray kitten calls out to him. "My name is Sadie. And who are you?"

"I'm Sam."

"Why did you come to a place like this? What do you want here?"

"I came to find something wonderful, but it doesn't look like it's here."

"If you want to find something wonderful, you'd better go someplace special," says Sadie, with a twinkle in her eye. "This is just perfect.

I want to find something wonderful too. Let's look together." Sadie starts walking away. Sam follows her.

"Is this a special place? Is there something wonderful here?" As they arrive at a train station, Sam is shocked again. "It's noisy, and I feel as if I'm going to be crushed by all the feet. It's the same as the street, isn't it!"

"To find someplace wonderful, you have to go on a journey—by train!"
With a straight face, Sadie keeps walking.

After sneaking through a ticket gate, the two of them come to a platform.
"Hide under that empty box, Sam!" says Sadie.
"Why?"

"You don't know anything, do you? Cats can't buy tickets, so we can only
ride the train by sneaking on."

Sam and Sadie get on the train without any problem.

"Do we still have to hide, Sadie?"

"Yes, we do. We'll be there soon, so be patient, Sam."

"It's very hard to go to a special place, isn't it?"

"Yes. But you have to go through hardship, to find anything wonderful."

Sam and Sadie keep whispering to each other under the empty box.

"This way, Sam! Hurry! Hurry!"
Sadie suddenly jumps off the train and starts running.
Sam runs too. They go through a fence.

"Oh, what a wonderful place!"
Sam and Sadie look around and find one wonderful thing after another.
"The sun is shining!"

"All the flowers are in bloom!"

"There's a nice breeze . . ."

"And there's a pond!"

Sadie starts walking. Sam starts walking, too.
"Where are we going, Sam?"

Sam answers, "Anywhere Sadie wants to go."
"I will go wherever you want to go, Sam," says Sadie.

"I've finally found what I was looking for. The special place I found is next to Sam. The something wonderful I found is Sam," says Sadie.

Sam answers, "I've found what I was looking for too. The special place
I found is next to Sadie. The something wonderful I found is Sadie."
The two look into each other's eyes.

"I'm so happy."

"Me too, Sam."

Sam sits next to Sadie, and Sadie sits next to Sam. They gaze at the moon all night long.

The next morning, the surprised artist shouts "Oh! Sam! What happened?"

But, after quietly looking at the painting for a while, the artist says, "I'm happy for you, Sam."

First edition for the United States and the Philippines published 1993 by
Barron's Educational Series, Inc.

First published 1991 by Kodansha Ltd.,
2—12—21 Otowa Bunkyo-ku,
Tokyo 112—01 Japan
© Masaru Mizobuti/Erika Tatihara, 1991
Illustrations: Masaru Mizobuti
Story: Erika Tatihara

International Standard Book No. 0-8120-1712-9 (P), 0-8120-6359-7 (H)

Library of Congress Catalog Card No. 93-739

Library of Congress Cataloging-in-Publication Data

Tachihara, Erika, 1937-
   [Boku no sagashimono. English]
   Picture purrfect kittens/by Erika Tatihara: illustrated by Masaru
Mizobuti.—1st ed.
     p.   cm
   Summary: One evening after an artist has left his studio, a kitten steps
out of a painting and sets off on an adventure in the city.
   ISBN 0-8120-6359-7   ISBN 0-8120-1712-9

   [1. Cats—Fiction.   2. Painting—Fiction.]   I. Mizobuti, Masaru, ill.
II. Title
PZ7.T1155Pi   1993   93-739
[E]—dc20   CIP
                                                          AC

PRINTED IN HONG KONG
3456 9927 987654321